LOVED PEOPLE LOVE PEOPLE

Written by Jessica Vander Leahy

Illustrated by Heymill

For everyone who has a body, a mind and a heart.

First published in 2021 by Tablo Publishing.

Level 1, 41-43 Stewart St, Richmond VIC 3121

www.tablo.com

21 22 23 LSC 10 9 8 7 6 5 4 3 2 1

Loved People Love People

Copyright © Jessica Vander Leahy and Heymill 2021

A catalogue record for this book is available from the National Library of Australia

ISBN: 9781649698902

Cover and interior design and illustrations by Heymill

LOVED PEOPLE LOVE PEOPLE

Written by Jessica Vander Leahy

Illustrated by Heymill

tablo

The firstest of first
things you should know,
Is no matter how big,
or small you may grow,

If you are lucky,
and long goes your life,
Your skin will stretch,
so you'll fit without strife.

Your body might scar,
blemish and crease,
But be grateful; it's a miracle
that one day will cease.

Through smooth skin to fuzz,
then hairy parts galore,
All these tiny wonders
you'll come to adore.

Lumps and bumps may
come and may go,
You're human after all,
they're part of the show.

Your body is a true
and wonderful gift,
The home in which
you'll always drift.

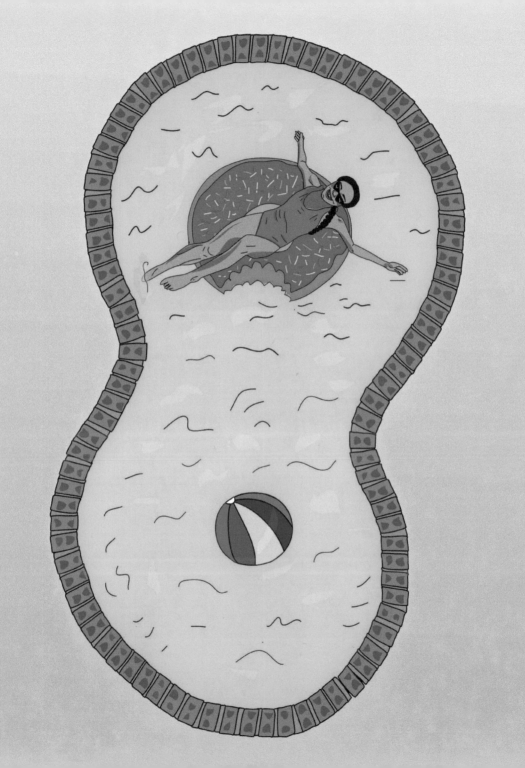

Sometimes you might
feel shy or ashamed,
Embarrassed or guilty,
and unwilling to change.

And there are times you
can act very silly indeed,
Trying to do better
is one way to succeed.

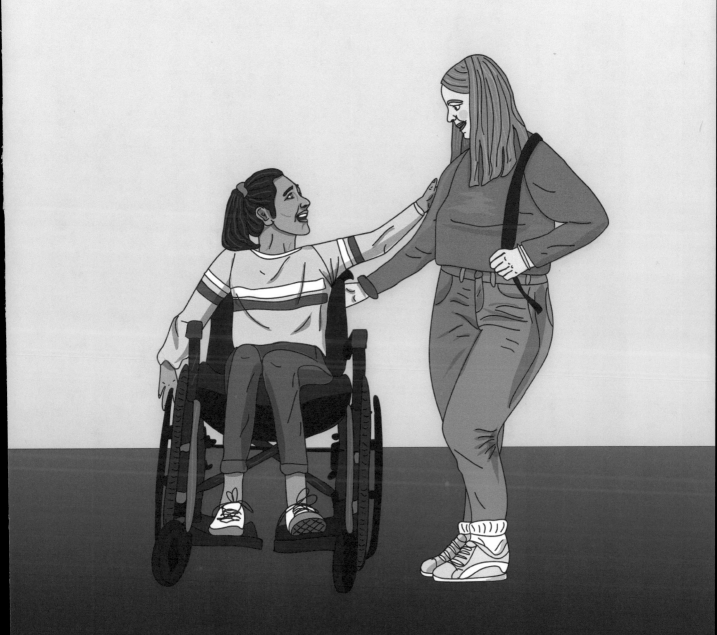

Though striving for better,
then bestest IS tough,
Know truly...

Doing your **BEST** is always **ENOUGH**

And if someone else tries
to make you feel small,
On the inside they mightn't
like themselves at all.

Bullies come armed with
their sticks and their stones.
Stand up for yourself!
Feel that courage in your bones!

But acknowledging hurt
doesn't make you a sook,
Sometimes tears are needed,
an inside look.

Forgiving yourself is a gift,
don't forget,
Forgiving others too,
you'll never regret.

So, keep remembering
you're worthy of this space.
Loving yourself should
take pride of place.

The lastest of last things
you should know,
Loved people love people,
that's the direction to grow.

Created by two mates

Jessica Vander Leahy is a model and writer currently living in Cavanbah/Byron Bay, Australia. She very much wants people to love themselves and each other.

Heymill is a whacky artist living in Naarm/Melbourne, Australia. She believes you can do anything you dream of, if you have the courage to try.

CPSIA information can be obtained
at www.ICGtesting.com
Printed in the USA
BVHW020111111121
621197BV00008B/835